Disney fairies

TinkerBell
AND THE
LOST TREASURE

ADAPTED BY
LISA MARSOLI

ILLUSTRATED BY
THE DISNEY STORYBOOK ARTISTS

DESIGNED BY
DEBORAH BOONE

PaRragon

Bath · New York · Singapore · Hong Kong · Cologne · Delhi · Melbourne

Summer was over. It was time for the fairies of Pixie Hollow to bring the beautiful season of autumn to the mainland! Unseen by the humans below, they burst through the clouds and began working their magic.

Soon the whole world was full of the warm colours of autumn. The fairies headed for the Second Star to the Right to make their journey home.

Back in Pixie Hollow, other fairies were collecting pixie dust from the Pixie Dust Tree. Pixie dust made it possible for all fairies to do their special kinds of magic.

When the buzzer signaling the end of the workday sounded, Terence bid his fellow dust-keepers goodbye. As usual, he was off to help his best friend, Tinker Bell, with her latest invention.

Terence found Tinker Bell at the stream putting the finishing touches on her new boat, the Pixie Dust Express. Soon she was ready for a test run. She launched the gourd boat into the water and Terence got into a leaf boat and paddled up beside her.

"Don't worry. I'll be right next to you," he said. "Let 'er rip!"

Tink pulled the rip cord and the Pixie Dust Express

zoomed away.

"Whoa!" cried Terence as a huge spray of water from Tink's boat sank his.

Tink sped along, pulling various levers. Suddenly, wings, skis and a waterwheel popped out, making her boat move forwards even faster.

"Uh-oh," Tink said as she spotted some rocks up ahead. The boat's skis snapped off, but her craft cruised ashore and kept on going – right towards a tree! The Pixie Dust Express shot up the tree's trunk, coming to rest on the tippy-top, then fell back to the ground.

"Are you okay?" asked Terence.

"I'm good, thanks," Tink assured him.

"Wow, I'm impressed," Terence said as he helpfully gathered the bits and pieces of her boat. "You're really handling this well."

But Tink couldn't hold her frustration in for long. "Aaargh!" she cried. "I can't believe the boat broke!"

"Ah, it just needs a little tinkering," Terence said breezily.

His cheerful attitude had Tinker Bell feeling better in no time.

Suddenly, a fairy arrived with a message. Queen Clarion
wanted to see Tinker Bell right away! Tink nervously hurried
to the royal chambers, where Queen Clarion, the Minister of
Autumn and Fairy Mary were waiting for her.

"Since time immemorial," the minister began solemnly, "fairies have celebrated the end of autumn with revelry – and this particular autumn coincides with a blue harvest moon. A new sceptre must be created to celebrate the occasion."

He led Tinker Bell to a hall filled with stunning sceptres, each one unique. "This year, it is the turn of the tinker fairies."

"And Fairy Mary has recommended you," Queen Clarion declared.

Tinker Bell gasped in disbelief.

"At the top of the sceptre you will place a moonstone," the minister continued. He directed everyone's attention to an ancient tapestry hanging on the wall. "When the blue moon is at its peak, its rays will pass through the gem, creating blue pixie dust. The blue pixie dust restores the Pixie Dust Tree."

"Here is the moonstone," said Fairy Mary as she led Tink to an ornate case. "It has been handed down from generation to generation. It is ridiculously fragile."

Tink was touched to be given such an honour. She hugged Fairy Mary – and knocked the moonstone out of its case!

"You have to be careful!" Fairy Mary cried. She caught the moonstone and placed it back in its case.

Tinker Bell gently took the case, bowed and left the chamber.

That night, Terence paid Tink a visit. She told him all about being chosen to create the new autumn sceptre.

"The blue moon only rises in Pixie Hollow every eight years," Terence explained. "The trajectory of the light beams have got to match the curvature of the moonstone at a ninety-degree angle so the light can transmute into pixie dust."

Tink was impressed with Terence's knowledge. When he volunteered to be her assistant, she was all for it!

Terence arrived at Tink's house bright and early the next day. She was still in bed.

"Mornin'," he called. "We have one full moon until the Autumn Revelry."

Terence left Tink a tasty breakfast and headed off to work. Later, on his way home, he dropped off some supplies he thought she might be able to use.

Day after day, Tink tried out different designs for the sceptre. And day after day, Terence was there with food, advice and a cheerful willingness to do any job that Tinker Bell wanted him to do. She couldn't have asked for a more helpful assistant.

As time wore on, though, Tink began to find Terence a bit too helpful. His broom scratched annoyingly on the floor when he swept. He got in her way when she was working. He sometimes stoked the fire so much that the room filled with smoke. Still, she tried to be patient.

Finally, the day came for Tink to finish her creation.

"Steady," said Terence as Tink removed the moonstone from its case.

"I know," replied Tink. "Shhh."

With Terence hovering over her, Tink manoeuvered the moonstone closer to the sceptre, but then a piece broke off the setting.

"Looks like you need some sort of sharp thingy," said Terence as Tink tried to repair it.

As he headed out the door to find a tool to do the job, Tink called, "Take your time!"

Once she was alone, Tink was able to concentrate and repair the setting. She placed the moonstone at the top of the sceptre.

Just then, Terence arrived, proudly rolling in a compass he had found at the cove.

"It's your sharp thingy," he announced.

Tink was annoyed. The compass was round – the exact opposite of sharp!

"Would you please get this thing out of here?" she said. She bumped the compass with her hip and it rolled across the room. WHACK! The compass hit the sceptre, causing the moonstone to pop out. Then the compass began to spin, finally tipping over and landing on the sceptre. Tink's beautiful creation shattered instantly.

Tink quickly grabbed the moonstone. "Out!" she yelled at Terence. "You brought this stupid thing here. This is your fault."

Terence was stunned. "Fine! Last time I try to help you!" he yelled back.

Tink set the moonstone down on a cushion and began to pace. She didn't know how she could fix the sceptre in time. In frustration, she kicked the compass with all her might. The cover popped open – and crushed the moonstone!

"No!" Tinker Bell said with a gasp.

That night, after failing to repair the moonstone, Tink desperately tried to figure out what to do next. Her friends Clank and Bobble stopped by.

"Came to see if you wanted to join us for Fairy-Tale Theatre," said Clank.

"I really don't have time," Tink answered nervously.

"Not to worry," Bobble told her. "We'll tell Fairy Mary you couldn't make it."

Suddenly, Tinker Bell realized that Fairy Mary might know where to find another moonstone.

21

So Tink went to the Fairy-Tale Theatre – but she just couldn't tell Fairy Mary she had broken the moonstone.

The show began. A fairy named Lyria appeared.

"'Twas a distant time ago when a pirate ship arrived in Never Land," she began. "The pirates searched until they found a fairy, and forced her to lead them to the enchanted Mirror of Incanta. Forged by fairy magic in ages past, the mirror had the power to grant three wishes."

Next, Lyria told how the pirates made only two wishes before being shipwrecked and losing the mirror forever.

Tink listened carefully. This magic mirror could be just what she needed! Lyria's story continued. "Journey due north past Never Land, till a faraway island is close at hand," she said. Tink was very excited to hear clues that could lead her to the pirate ship and the magic mirror. Lyria spoke of an arch of stone and an old troll bridge. Tink's head was so full of directions and clues, she didn't pay attention. She thought Lyria had said "toll bridge"!

Lyria went on, explaining that hidden deep inside the ship, amid gems and gold, was the mirror. Pretending to be tired, Tink left the theatre as quickly as she could. She had to find that mirror and use that last wish to restore the moonstone!

Back at home, Tink quickly drew a map of the lost island, consulted the compass and began to pack some supplies.

"How am I going to carry all this?" she wondered.

Still, she kept packing. "Not enough," she decided as she checked her bag of pixie dust. But Tink wasn't worried. She'd figure out a way to get more.

But the next morning, Tink couldn't talk anyone into giving her more pixie dust. Not knowing where else to turn, she went to Terence and bluntly told him what she needed.

"That's why you're here?" Terence asked. He had been expecting an apology for the way Tink had yelled at him. "Why do you need more dust?"

"A true friend wouldn't ask," said Tink angrily.

"A true friend wouldn't ask me to break the rules!" Terence replied.

"Then I guess we're not true friends," shot back Tink.

"I guess we're not," replied Terence.

Even though Tink didn't think she had enough pixie dust for her journey, she stubbornly moved ahead with her plan. First, she had to design and build a vehicle that could carry her and all of her supplies to the lost island.

Tinker Bell expertly assembled what looked like a hot-air balloon from a gourd, a bunch of cotton balls, and an array of pots and pans – all in less than a day!

She dressed in her adventurer's outfit and, at dusk, she sprinkled the balloon with pixie dust and lifted off with the moonstone fragments safely tucked in her bag.

"So long, Pixie Hollow!" Tinker Bell called as she rose higher and higher into the sky. "I'll be back soon."

As night fell, Tinker Bell watched a bat chasing a glowing mass of fireflies towards the balloon. Luckily, they passed by without causing any trouble.

A little while later, she went to have a snack – and discovered an empty supply bag and a very full firefly!

She lifted her visitor out of the bag. "Shoo! Go find your friends," she ordered. "I'm on a very important mission."

Tink tried to get rid of the firefly by hurling a stick for him to fetch, but he soon returned. The stick caught on her bag of pixie dust and flung it out of the balloon!

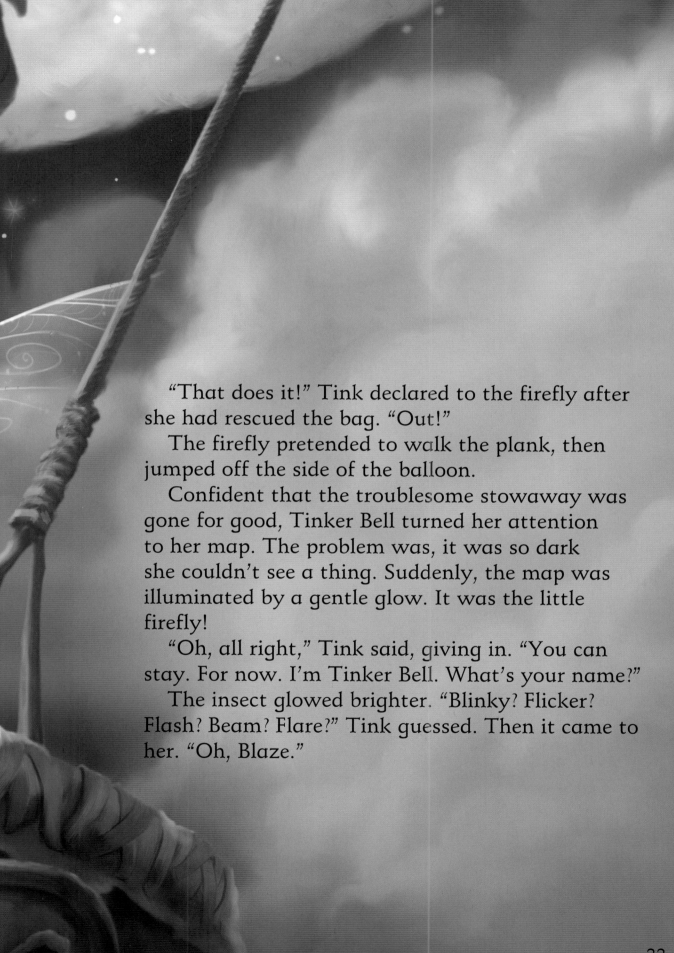

"That does it!" Tink declared to the firefly after she had rescued the bag. "Out!"

The firefly pretended to walk the plank, then jumped off the side of the balloon.

Confident that the troublesome stowaway was gone for good, Tinker Bell turned her attention to her map. The problem was, it was so dark she couldn't see a thing. Suddenly, the map was illuminated by a gentle glow. It was the little firefly!

"Oh, all right," Tink said, giving in. "You can stay. For now. I'm Tinker Bell. What's your name?"

The insect glowed brighter. "Blinky? Flicker? Flash? Beam? Flare?" Tink guessed. Then it came to her. "Oh, Blaze."

Tinker Bell and Blaze anxiously kept watch for land until they flew into a fogbank. In the morning, when the fog cleared, the travellers discovered they were stuck in a tree.

"This must be the lost island," Tink decided as she looked around. "And there it is! The stone arch from the story. You stay here and guard the balloon. I'll be right back."

Tink jubilantly flew towards the stone arch. But when she got closer, she saw that it was just the entwined branches of two trees.

Meanwhile, the balloon was starting to drift away! Blaze tried to warn Tink, but she was distracted. By the time he got her attention, the balloon was gone.

"My compass!" yelled Tink. "My supplies! My pixie dust! Why didn't you warn me?"

The pair raced off to find the balloon. Before they had got very far, though, Tink collided with a tree, and everything went black. Blaze sent out a distress call, and within minutes bugs arrived carrying food and water for the injured fairy.

Tink immediately felt better and asked the bugs to lead her to the stone arch. She tried to fly after them, but she couldn't lift off. "I'm out of dust," she realized. "Guess I'll be walking from here."

As they made their way to the arch, Tink stumbled upon her compass where it had fallen from the balloon. She never would have found it if it weren't for her new little friends.
Tink suddenly realized how much she missed her old friend Terence.

Back in Pixie Hollow, Terence missed Tink, too. That night, he shared his dilemma with a wise old owl.

"Tink is my best friend. We should just forgive each other," Terence admitted. "Someone just needs to take the first step."

"Who?" asked the owl.

"I think it should be Tink," Terence answered. "She shouldn't have treated me that way."

"Who?" the owl repeated.

It seemed to Terence that the owl was trying to make a point. "Me!" he said suddenly.

Terence flew straight to Tink's house and knocked on the door. There was no answer. "Anyone home?" Terence called as he stepped inside. He felt something crunch under his feet.

"The moonstone!" he gasped.

Investigating further, he discovered the diagram of Tink's balloon and the supply list for her trip. Terence knew that wherever his friend was, she could use some help!

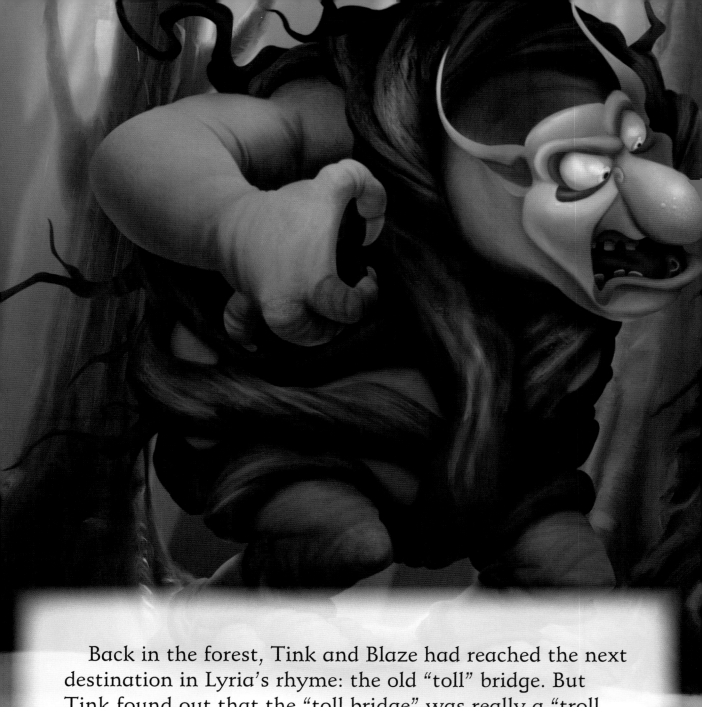

Back in the forest, Tink and Blaze had reached the next destination in Lyria's rhyme: the old "toll" bridge. But Tink found out that the "toll bridge" was really a "troll bridge," and the trolls weren't co-operating.

"Beat it before we grind your bones to make our bed," said the small troll.

"Make our bread," corrected the tall troll. The small troll got angry, and soon the two were having a heated argument.

They were so busy squabbling that they didn't even notice when Tink and Blaze tiptoed over the bridge!

The two explorers continued across the island and into scrub land. Finally, they emerged from the scrub land onto a beautiful beach. Tink was overjoyed. She had found the pirates' shipwreck!

"Okay, Blaze, this is it! We've got to find that mirror and fix the moonstone. Let's go!"

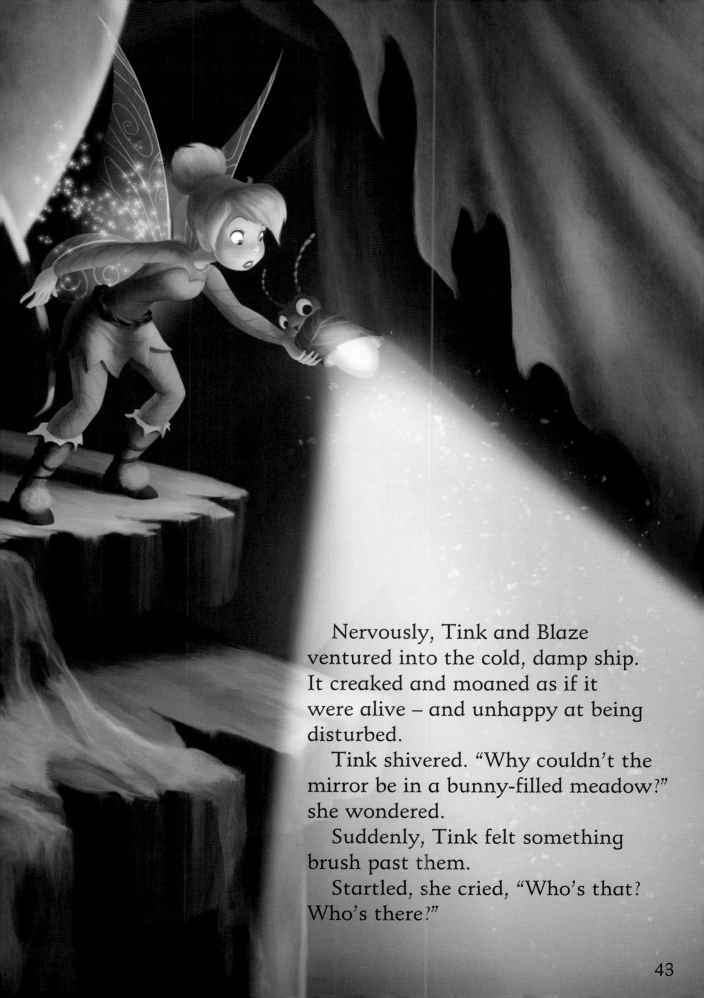

Nervously, Tink and Blaze
ventured into the cold, damp ship.
It creaked and moaned as if it
were alive – and unhappy at being
disturbed.

Tink shivered. "Why couldn't the
mirror be in a bunny-filled meadow?"
she wondered.

Suddenly, Tink felt something
brush past them.

Startled, she cried, "Who's that?
Who's there?"

Despite their rising fear, the pair continued on to the captain's quarters.

"Look, Blaze," said Tink. There, illuminated by a shaft of light, was a bag. Did it hold the gems and gold that Lyria had spoken of? Tinker Bell pulled out the compass needle and hurled it at the bag. RIIIP! Lost fairy treasure spilled out into a heap on the floor.

Tink reached into the treasure, feeling around and pulled out – the mirror!

She laid the fragments of the moonstone in front of the mirror, then took a deep breath. "I've only got one shot at this," she told herself.

"I wish …," she began, but she was distracted by Blaze's buzzing near her ear. She tried again.

"I wish…" Blaze continued his racket.

BZZZZZ!

"Blaze, I wish you'd be quiet for one minute!" Tinker Bell shouted.

The buzzing stopped.

Tinker Bell gasped. "No, that one didn't count!" she wailed. Her one chance to fix the moonstone was gone.

As one of her tears fell onto the mirror, Terence's face appeared in the reflection.

"Terence!" Tink exclaimed. "I am so sorry."

"I forgive you," replied Terence, "but why didn't you tell me about the moonstone?"

"I didn't think I needed any help," Tink explained. "I was wrong. I wish you were here with me."

"I am with you," said Terence. He was standing right behind her! Tinker Bell ran to her friend. They were so happy to see each other!

"How did you...," Tink began.

"I flew all night and all day over the sea," Terence explained. "And just when I was going to run out of dust, I stumbled into that flying machine of yours. I only had a pinch of dust left. It got me all the way here."

"But where did you even find the dust to make it this far?" Tink asked.

"I...uh...'borrowed' a little extra," Terence admitted.

Tink couldn't believe Terence had broken the rules for her!

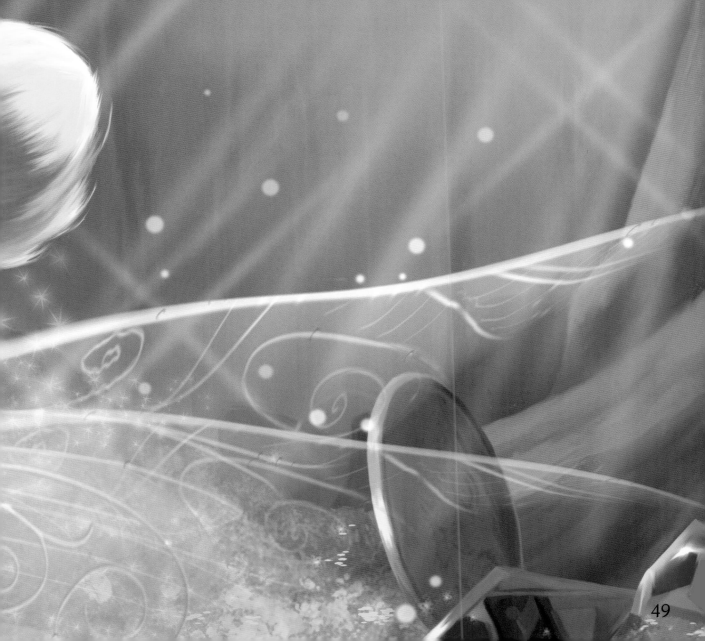

Just then, the friends' joyful reunion was interrupted. A vicious pack of rats had come to make a meal of the fairies!

Tink and Terence grabbed the mirror and ran. Blaze tried to distract the rodents by darting and dipping overhead. But it was no use. Terence and Tink were soon surrounded. Thinking quickly, Terence grabbed Tink and swung across the room. CRASH! The pair landed on a stack of plates, then rode one through the air like a flying saucer. Suddenly, Terence spotted a loose board in the floor.

"There's our way out," he told Tink. While she tried to pry the board open, Terence held off the rats by brandishing the compass needle like a sword. But when he lost his weapon, the rats began to close in!

Suddenly, the shadow of a hideous monster appeared on the wall behind Terence. It growled ferociously, sending the rats scurrying away in fear. Tink and Blaze cheered. They had made the "creature" with Blaze's light – and its growls by using Tink's hat as a megaphone!

"C'mere, you vicious monster!" said Tink, giving the tiny firefly a playful rub on the head.

Terence led Tink and Blaze back to the balloon. Luckily, there was just enough pixie dust left in Tink's bag to allow them to lift off.

"I don't know if it will help, but I brought this," said Terence. He handed Tink the shattered sceptre.

"Hey, I've got an idea," Tink announced to Terence. "Would you help me?"

Together, they worked through the night to repair the broken sceptre as the blue moon rose higher in the sky.

Back in Pixie Hollow, the revelry was already under way. But where, Fairy Mary wondered, was Tinker Bell? "The blue harvest moon is high. The moonbeams are almost at their mark. This is a disaster!" she moaned.

Suddenly, Tink and Terence swept in, waving and smiling from Tink's balloon.

Queen Clarion was impressed. "Now, that's an entrance!" she exclaimed.

Tink walked over and kneeled in front of the queen. "Your Highness," she said with great ceremony.

"Where is the sceptre?" Queen Clarion asked.

"Uh...there were...complications," Tinker Bell replied.

A look of dread passed over the faces of Fairy Mary and Queen Clarion.

"But it's ready now, Your Highness," added Tink as Terence handed her the sceptre.

"Fairies of Pixie Hollow," Tink announced as she placed the sceptre in a special stand. "I present the Autumn Sceptre."

Tink removed the leaf covering – and everyone gasped. Her creation was fashioned from the broken bits of the sceptre, the bent mirror frame, and fragments of the moonstone. It was beautiful – and wildly unusual.

"Please work, please work, please work," Tinker Bell whispered as the rays from the blue moon began to touch the sceptre.

WHOOSH! The moonbeams reflected everywhere and streaked above the crowd, raining down rare blue pixie dust.

At first a flurry, then a shower, then a blizzard, the dust swirled in the air before settling in drifts on the ground.

"Your Majesty!" the Minister of Autumn cried jubilantly. "I've never seen this much blue pixie dust before!"

Fairy Mary agreed. "It's at least a million smidges. Maybe more."

Tinker Bell's fairy friends Silvermist, Fawn, Iridessa and Rosetta were amazed. "Only Tinker Bell," Iridessa said affectionately.

"Fairies of Pixie Hollow," Queen Clarion said. "Tonight, I believe, is our finest revelry ever, thanks to one very special fairy – Tinker Bell."

Tink pulled Terence close to her and tried to get the queen's attention. "And her friend Terence," added Queen Clarion.

Then Blaze flew between Tink and Terence. The queen continued, "And her new friend..."

"Blaze," Tink said.

All the fairies cheered and applauded.

The Minister of Autumn handed Tink the sceptre. "All right, everyone, to the Pixie Dust Tree," he announced as Tinker Bell led the procession.

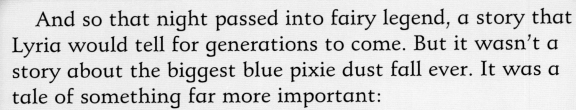

And so that night passed into fairy legend, a story that Lyria would tell for generations to come. But it wasn't a story about the biggest blue pixie dust fall ever. It was a tale of something far more important:

The greatest treasures are not gold,
Nor jewels, nor works of art.
They cannot be held in your hands.
They're held within your heart.
Worldly things will fade away
And seasons come and go,
But the treasure of true friendship
Will never lose its glow.